To: _____

From: _____

Date: _____

**This book is for Danielle Malina-Jones,
her husband, Harold, and her children, Julian, Julianna, and Jacob**
— *Anthony DeStefano*

To Hayla Grace, with much love
— *Richard Cowdrey*

. . .

Published by Servant
An imprint of Franciscan Media
28 W. Liberty St.
Cincinnati, OH 45202
www.AmericanCatholic.org

Printed in the United States of America.
Printed on acid-free paper.
15 16 17 18 19 5 4 3 2 1

The Puppy That No One Wanted

Anthony DeStefano

Illustrated by Richard Cowdrey
New York Times Bestselling Artist

• • •

The woman said to Jesus:

"'Lord, even the dogs under the table eat the children's crumbs.'
Then Jesus answered her, 'Woman, great is your faith!
Let it be done for you as you wish.'"

— Mark 7:28; Matthew 15:28 (NRSV)

• • •

"I wish someone had given a dog to Jesus."

– Rudyard Kipling

• • •

servant
AN IMPRINT OF
FRANCISCAN MEDIA
Cincinnati, Ohio

Once upon a time, there was a poor, mangy, smelly little puppy. He was the runt of the litter, and from the moment he was born, he was cast aside and forced to live on his own.

Many days, he would wander through the muddy streets of town, cold and hungry, looking for something to eat. But wherever he went, people gave him nasty looks and yelled, "Get out of here, you dirty mutt! There's no food for you here."

Still, he managed to be a cheerful puppy. He survived on whatever scraps he could find and never lost hope that one day he would find a home.

2

At night he slept in an alley with the other stray dogs. Some of them were old and sick, and in the winter they all huddled together for warmth. Often the puppy would try to lift their spirits by making them laugh.

When he fell asleep, the puppy always had the same dream. He dreamed about running through a beautiful, open field of flowers, under a warm, sunlit sky. And of course, he dreamed about food. Lots of food!

4

When he woke up, he was always starving. The other dogs would be hungry too, but they were too weak to go looking for food. So the puppy would have to go off alone.

One day, after searching for hours and being chased away by many people, his nose caught a whiff of something delicious. It was coming from the home of the town butcher. It smelled heavenly, and the puppy just had to find out what it was. So he sneaked into the house and saw the butcher sitting at his kitchen table having lunch. The puppy's mouth watered as he watched the man eating a juicy steak.

Slowly the puppy crept through the man's legs and under the table. There were a few scraps on the floor and the puppy hungrily ate them. *"If only the man would drop some more food,"* the puppy hoped.

Suddenly the man stopped eating. "What is that AWFUL smell?" he yelled. Then he looked down and shouted, "Why you dirty, stinky mutt, what are you doing under my table? Get out of here before I make dog stew out of you!"

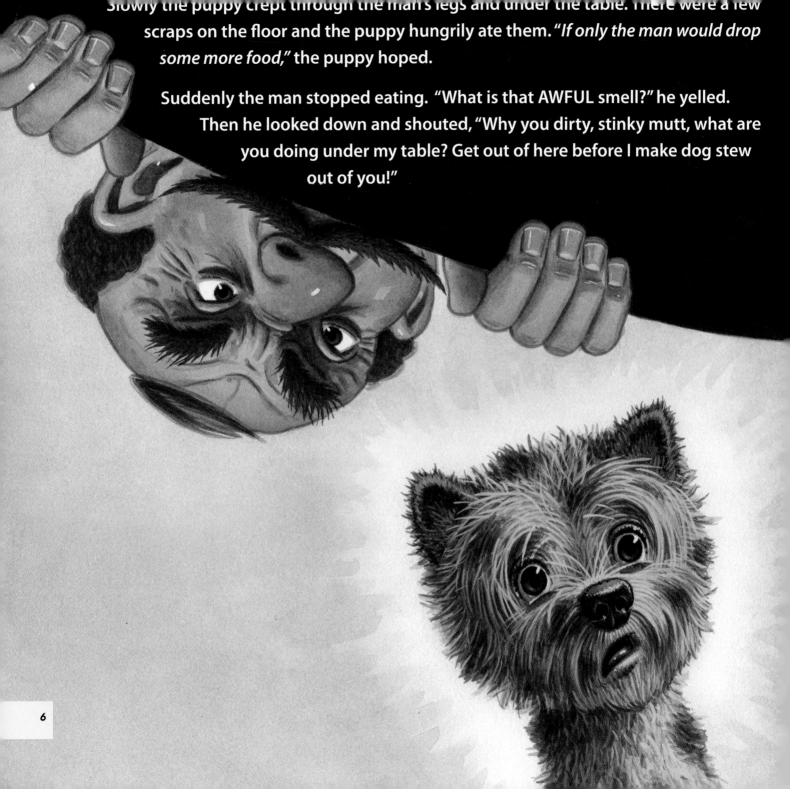

The butcher tried to kick the puppy, but he managed to escape through the window. He ran as fast as he could down the street, but the butcher threw the steak bone at him, barely missing his head.

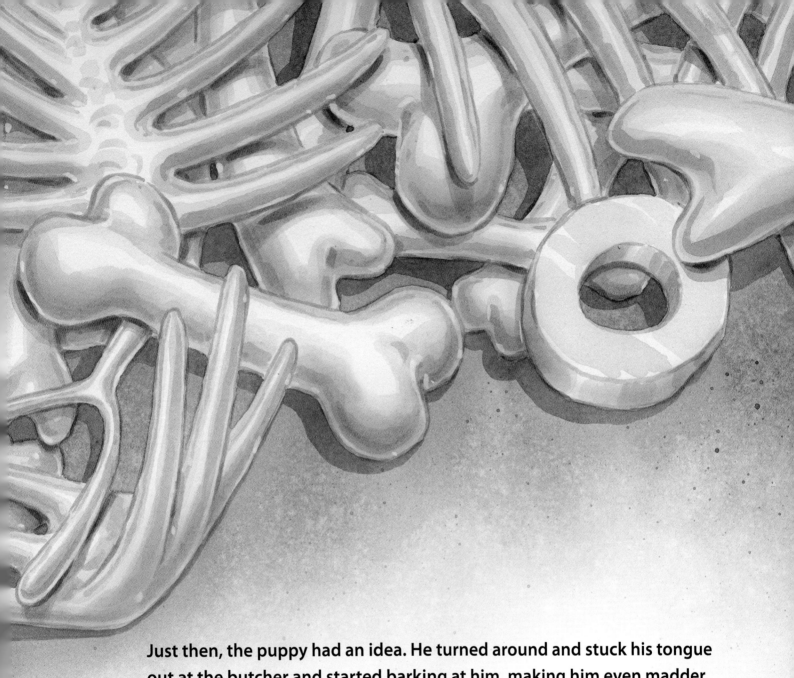

Just then, the puppy had an idea. He turned around and stuck his tongue out at the butcher and started barking at him, making him even madder. The butcher threw another bone at him, and then another, and another. Every time a bone came flying at him, the puppy dodged out of the way. Soon, the man got tired of throwing bones and slammed his window shut, yelling, "Don't you ever come back here again, you smelly little runt!"

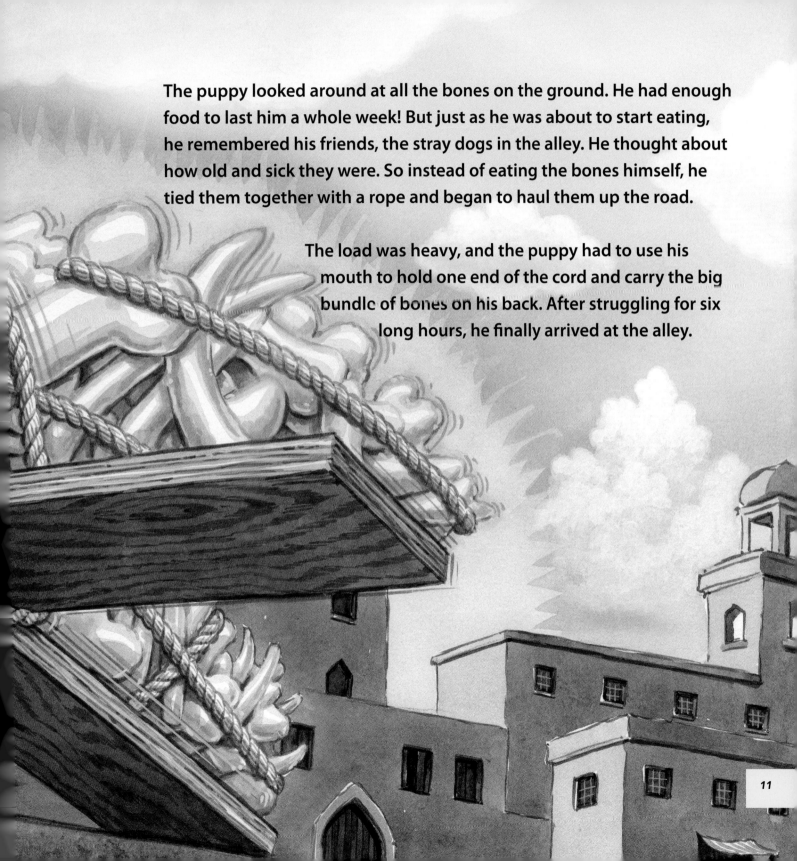

The puppy looked around at all the bones on the ground. He had enough food to last him a whole week! But just as he was about to start eating, he remembered his friends, the stray dogs in the alley. He thought about how old and sick they were. So instead of eating the bones himself, he tied them together with a rope and began to haul them up the road.

The load was heavy, and the puppy had to use his mouth to hold one end of the cord and carry the big bundle of bones on his back. After struggling for six long hours, he finally arrived at the alley.

11

The other dogs couldn't believe all the food he had brought. They were so hungry they dove past the puppy onto the pile of bones, devouring it as fast as they could. The puppy just watched as they ate and ate, and when they were finished, there wasn't a trace left. As soon as they were done eating, the dogs fell asleep, happy and satisfied. But the puppy was still starving. Even though he was exhausted, he had to go out again to search for food. And to make matters even worse, it had started to rain.

12

Walking through the streets of the town in the pouring rain, the puppy was sad and wet and cold. Everything was so muddy! There wasn't a crumb of food to be found anywhere. Just then—at the end of the road—the puppy saw some light coming from the window of a small house. He climbed up and peered inside.

13

What he saw made his heart beat faster. For inside was a family seated around a table. There was a man, his wife, and a little boy—and they were having dinner. The puppy watched as they said a prayer and began eating. The house seemed so toasty warm. Looking closer, he saw that a piece of hot, crusty bread had fallen on the floor next to the boy's feet. Taking a chance, the puppy jumped to the ground and sneaked into the house.

When no one was looking, the puppy darted across the floor. Trying not to make a sound, he quickly ate the bread. Then he waited to see if any more crumbs would fall. But before he had a chance to eat anything else, the man above him said, "What is that AWFUL smell?" *"Now I'm in trouble,"* the puppy thought. When he looked up, he saw the little boy staring at him. "It's a puppy who's trying to eat scraps from the table," the boy said. Then, lifting him up, he asked, "What's the matter, little dog? Haven't you eaten anything today?"

The puppy wanted to tell the boy how hungry he was because he had given all his food away, but since he couldn't talk, he just yelped. The boy looked at him strangely and smiled— as though he somehow understood.

Then the boy's mother said, "He's a very smelly pup. Let's get him cleaned up."

So she put some warm, soapy water into a large wooden basin and handed the puppy to the boy, who started to wash him.

Afterward, the woman gave the puppy a huge plate of food. The puppy couldn't believe how tasty it was. While he was eating, the man said, "He can stay here tonight because of the storm. But tomorrow we'll have to decide what to do with him."

That night, the puppy slept in bed with the little boy. He watched the boy say his prayers and then snuggled up next to him. Imitating the boy, the puppy said a short prayer of his own: "Please, God, let me stay here with this nice family." Then he drifted off to asleep.

And he slept and slept and slept. He dreamed all night about the field of flowers. He was still sleeping when morning came and he heard the boy's voice: "Rise and shine, little dog. It's time to wake up."

22

The puppy wondered what was going to happen to him. Would he be thrown out again, like all the other times in his life? Would he be cast aside and forgotten? But the boy just looked at him and said, "Follow me."

So the puppy got up and trotted behind the boy and the man as they left the house and started walking down the road. Soon they came to a small shop on the edge of town.

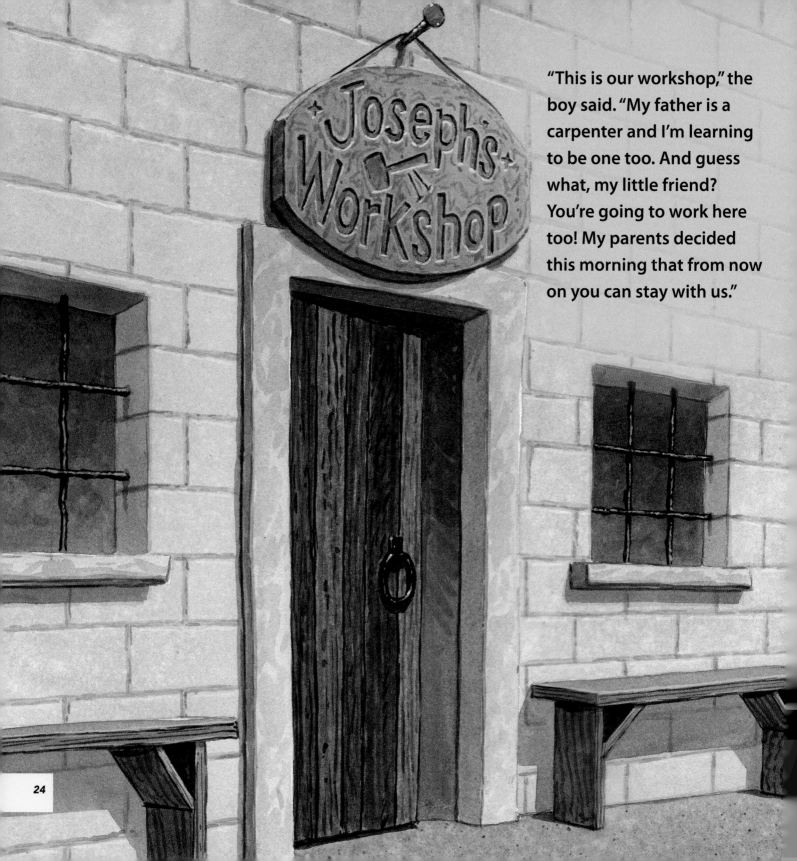

"This is our workshop," the boy said. "My father is a carpenter and I'm learning to be one too. And guess what, my little friend? You're going to work here too! My parents decided this morning that from now on you can stay with us."

The puppy couldn't contain his excitement. He started jumping up and down, yelping for joy. Could it really be that he finally had a home?

The boy showed him the shop. It was full of tools and nails and interesting things made of wood.

The puppy looked around in amazement. *"Imagine all the wonderful things that could be made here,"* he thought.

In back of the shop was a door that led to a yard. When the puppy went through, his eyes opened wide. For behind the shop was a huge, open field of flowers. He sat there for a long time looking at the flowers and the rolling hills and the sparrows flying high above in the sunshine.

The boy patted his head softly. "It's a field of lilies," he said. "Isn't it the most beautiful thing you've ever seen?" The puppy just nodded and licked the boy's hand.

And from that moment on the puppy lived with the family and was happy.

The man and the boy even built a row of cozy little doghouses beside the field of flowers for all the dogs in the alley, so they would never be cold again.

And forever after, the puppy belonged to the little boy—and he was the best, most faithful servant that any boy or girl could ever have.